Clay Faces Gloria's Ultimatum

Clay Faces
Gloria's Ultimatum

GEORGE MILLS

ISBN: 978-1-964462-89-9 (sc)
ISBN: 978-1-964462-90-5 (e)

Rev. date: 08/20/2024

"Clay Faces Gloria's Ultimatum"

It gives me great satisfaction to once again bring to you another one of Clay's adventures. Within these pages, you will get to meet Clay's friends, who have helped make his search for his be lovely wildflower a journey he won't forget anytime soon. Clay will be the one doing the narrating of his story.

Clay, are you ready to start telling your story if so, take it away.

"Afternoon in the Park"

As I sit here in the park thinking about the situation I've once again found myself in. I must decide between Mary Ann and Gloria. I feel deep within my heart that my world is once again being torn in half by these two lovely ladies whom I know very little about.

Although Mary Ann appears to be a God-fearing woman who puts her family first and does not seek center stage for herself, she's very selfless. Just last week, I was on my way to the grocery store to pick something up for Mrs. Mary. I saw her in the distance helping an elderly person at the grocery store. Others just look down their noses at the person and walk by. I'm not sure what you may think but, in my opinion, that speaks volumes about her character.

She is one of the sweetest people I've met so far in this desolate, desert town outside of Jimi of course. As I sit here with my face in my hands staring at the ground, I'm thinking back to a time not so long ago. I hear people talking as they come towards me. I look up to see who it could be and it's Amanda and her friend Jane.

I said, "Hello, Amanda, how are you and Jane doing today?"

Amanda answered, "Clay, we're tired from our two-mile jog. Would you mind if we sat down here beside you for a few minutes?"

I then answered, "Not at all Amanda. Amanda, can I ask you something?"

Amanda said "Sure Clay, what is on your mind?"

I then asked, "Amanda, I would like you to tell me the story behind your beautiful name because I feel deep down the need to escape from my own reality here."

"Well Clay, the story behind my name goes like this. My mom said that the night that my dad proposed to her, the song Amanda by Boston was playing on the jukebox at the café where they were having dinner. After mom accepted dad's proposal, they adopted it as their love song. This was a reminder of their love for one another. She went on to say that they promised to name their first daughter after that song. "

I thought, "Amanda", I love that song myself, and I can see why they chose it as a reminder of their love for one another.

I then asked, "Just out of curiosity, do you think that your dad may have asked someone to play that song because he was planning on proposing to her? "

She answered, "You know I never thought about him doing that, but he could have. Mom said he was a very romantic guy back in his younger days. You know, now that I think back to those days, she told me that not too long after they married, he would send her flowers to the place where she worked every Thursday. She proceeded to say Thursday while at work, her brother-in law stopped by to pick-up her sister for lunch. He saw her walking out the door with the flowers and asked if Matt (that was my dad's name) had done something wrong. Mom said my aunt Julie just looked at him and said why would you think that he did something wrong? Not every man who sends his wife flowers has done something wrong. She gets flowers once a week because Matt wants to let her know how much he loves her".

I told her, "Amanda, I must say your dad sounds like a great man. Only if I had a lovely woman in my life who loves me, I too would send flowers to show her my love and affection. I would also show her that I'm always thinking of her. I thought of this song by Ronnie Milsap entitled Daydreams About Night Things. Have you heard that song?

Amanda answered, "Yes Clay, I've heard it and it's one of my all-time favorite songs of his along with (There's No Getting Over Me").

I agreed, "Oh yes, I love that one as well. Jane, who is your favorite singer?"

Jane answered, "Clay, if I told you who I love listening to, you would start laughing".

I challenge her, "Why don't you just tell me and see if I'll laugh? "

Jane continued, "Okay then, I love listening to the Bellamy Brothers. Now as for my favorite song of theirs, it would be, ("If I said you had a beautiful body would you hold it again for me?").

"Yes, that is a great song, one that takes me back to a time I won't ever forget." I replied.

Jane continued, "Oh really, would you like to explain?"

I answered, "No!" "I would not. Let's change the subject. Now why are you both laughing?"

Jane responded, "Clay, I'm laughing because of the look on your face when you said No. Which makes me think that you're trying to hide a good story".

"If you're not going to tell us, I'm going to make one for you".

"No, don't Jane!".

Amanda finally said, "Clay, Jane won't, but I will".

"Amanda, if you think that you can then go for it, I would like to hear what you come up with. "

"I can visualize you standing in front of a full-size mirror singing that song, as you're singing it to this beautiful woman with whom you like".

"Hmm, I will not agree nor disagree with that statement. Now can we please change the subject?

"Okay then, what have you been doing besides sitting here watching squirrels play?"

"Well, Jane, to answer your question, I've been enjoying the peaceful surroundings of this beautiful park and I'm reminiscing back to a time that has long gone. I'm thinking until you bring up that song".

"Clay, please tell us you weren't thinking about Jimi again".

"She is a beautiful woman from a different time in my life. You see, the story goes like this. Shortly after my divorce, she was the first woman who came into my shattered life. She gave it a new meaning during that difficult time. She became that great friend whom I could lean on. Even though she now resides in a time long past, she will always have a special place in my heart. She was the light that illuminated my darkest hours during that time. She was there for me when I needed someone in my life, but she left out the most important part that was missing from my heart."

"Clay, what part did she leave out?"

"Jane, the part that fills the void of love."

"Well, Clay my friend, it has been nice seeing you again, but we must head on over to the gym to finish our workout."

"Okay Amanda, don't overdo your workout."

"Oh! No need to worry about us doing that! Bye for now."

"Bye ladies!"

In our last conversation, as we walked along the oceanfront early Monday morning, Mary Ann told me that she loved me for who I am. Now that is a big plus for someone like me. This is because when I first started out on this new journey looking for my beautiful wildflower, that kind of love only seemed to exist in my dreams.

I did not believe I could ever find that kind of love again. She is such a beautiful wildflower and for her to say she loves me just the way I am is a great reward. For some of us, we may never find that other person who holds the other half of our heart and that makes us feel whole in life. I once felt what it meant to feel whole in life.

However, after going through a divorce that shattered my life, I'm not so sure anymore. It all feels as if I've been awoken from this deep, dark dream and I find myself living in a different kind of world. I am unable to understand this new world of love and how it works. It seems very different from the world I grew up in. I feel I have to ask this question in the first place. If you can't find it in yourself to love someone for who they truly are, how can you admit you love that person? This is a question I may never answer.

Now as far as Gloria is concerned, she is also a sweet, lovely lady that seems to be a bit more demanding in many ways. This doesn't sit well with me. I don't know about you but I'm not looking for someone to be a mother-figure in a relationship. I don't mean that in a negative way so don't take it that way.

I've learned from my own failed relationship that it requires communication and compromise. You must take the time to talk things out in a relationship because each person can't have things in their own way every time. It doesn't work that way. It takes both people to find the right solution to their relationship. When a couple does that, along with being active in a church, I believe the relationship will be an absolute success.

Understand, I know that we all have our own unique personalities and that's what makes us stand apart from one another. Now, can you imagine a world filled with people with the same personalities? That would be a world filled with unhappy people.

As I continue to contemplate how I'll tell Gloria that I can no longer see her, Mary Ann has now admitted to me that she wants to share her life with me and no one else but the Lord. She also said she would not be upset with me if I chose Gloria over her. She just wants to see me be happy once again.

"Lord, you know that has always been my lifelong dream of finding such true love as hers. Oh Lord, may I ask you again what I should do here? I never expected to find myself in a difficult situation like this again. For there is no way I can be with them both; that goes against my beliefs learned from your word. According to Your word, marriage should be between one man and one woman. As I read in K.J.V., Matthew chapter 19, starting with verse 4 and going through verse 6. "And he answered and said, Have ye not read, that he who made them from the beginning made them male and female, and said, For this cause shall a man leave his father and mother, and shall cleave to his wife; and the two shall become one flesh?"

Lord, I can't reach deep enough into my own heart to find the right words to tell Gloria how I truly feel right now. You know she has this peculiar way of looking at me that takes my breath away. When our eyes lock together, just thinking that it's going to make it that much more difficult for me to tell her about Mary Ann. Lord, I am certain deep within my heart that no matter what the outcome may be, you will be there by my side. You have never let me down. Lord before we go over, there is just one more thing that I would like to say and that is You've never gone against the will of Your people even though they have gone against Your will time after time. Lord, why am I saying this? Well, it's because I myself feel that I've let You down in so many ways during the past seven years. I am sorry for not becoming the person You needed me to be.

Coffeeshop

After leaving the park to head over to see Gloria, I make one last stop at the coffee shop for a cup of Sue's delicious hot coffee. As I walk through the door, Sue stands behind the counter.

"Hello Sue, how are you this afternoon?"

"Well hello Clay, I'm doing great and thanks for asking. What brings you today? Can I get you something?" "Yes Sue, I will have a cup of coffee."

"So, Clay what have you been up to today?"

"Oh Sue, I've been sitting in the park thinking about how my life has changed."

"Hum now Clay, may I ask how has your life changed?"

"Well Sue, you know that life threw me into a whirlwind during my divorce. Some would say that I didn't even know if I was coming or leaving. For the life I once knew was shredded because of the divorce."

"Yes Clay, I know that heartache very well myself. Have you forgotten that I, myself have suffered from betrayal?"

"No Sue, I haven't forgotten about your divorce. Now Sue just when I thought I'd finally gotten over that difficult time in my life and got everything back on the right path for the first time in a long time. I once again feel like I'm back where I came from."

"Well Clay, may I ask why that is?"

"Sue, you may not know, but Mary Ann came by Mr. John's this past Monday morning to apologize for her rude, inappropriate behavior Monday night. While she was doing so, I asked her if she would mind walking with me down the oceanfront. Now before I realized what was going on, we were talking about how we're having these strong feelings towards one another. But Sue, here is where things become mind-boggling for me."

"Oh, how is that?" Well Sue, it's like this. Gloria and I have been talking as well and I think you already knew that part from seeing us last Monday evening."

"Yes, Clay, I saw you both having dinner together."

"Well Sue, what you don't know is that very evening Gloria and I took a long walk down by the ocean where we started kissing and having a very enjoyable time. She then gave me an ultimatum."

"Clay, before you go any further let me stop you right there, and please don't get mad at me for doing so."

"Now Sue, why would I get mad at you?"

"Clay, Mary Ann has told me about this already."

"Did she stop by here on her way home?"

"Yes, Clay, she did. She felt the need to talk to someone about her feelings about you. She also told me that she had stopped by Mr. Johns to see you. Before she could apologize for her rudeness, you asked her to join you for a walk down by the ocean. You two had a heart-to-heart talk."

"Oh, she did, did she!!?"

"Yes Clay".

"Well did she also tell you about how my feelings for her had grown stronger?" "Yes Clay, she told me that you said you felt that it all started the night she came on to you in the parking-lot, the night we all had dinner at Mr. John's. Clay, I'll tell you like I told her. I'm happy for you both but I believe you both deserve to be happy for once in your life."

"Thank you Sue. I hope the man of your dreams walks into your life."

Sue then thinks: ("Oh if you only knew! I once believed that he had but now he has confessed his love for my best friend!".)

"What were you thinking about Sue?"

"I was thinking that I should just give up on ever finding my true love."

"Now why would you say that, Sue?"

"Clay as you well know from your own search for true love, today's love is unlike the love of time past."

"Sue, you've got me confused now more than ever."

"The only way I can explain it is to say that people seem to have put more emphasis on making it more about themselves than actually taking time to love anyone else."

"Wait, I'm not sure I fully understand where you're coming from. Would you mind explaining it more in-depth and can I please have another cup of coffee?"

"Yes, you can have another cup of coffee."

"Thank you! Now please explain your analysis of love not being like our parents' love when we were growing up?"

"Clay, I'm not sure if I can explain it to you in a way you understand. For me it's very complicated in so many different ways."

"Yes, I understand what you mean about things being complicated. I'm not sure how I'll tell Gloria about Mary Ann."

"Clay, why don't you be truthful and let her know how you feel? That way she should be grateful and not hate you for breaking her tender heart."

"Thanks for the advice, you just made it that much harder. It's not like I would lie to her."

"No, Clay, that's not what I meant. I didn't mean to sound like you were lying to her. What I was trying to say was just let her know how you truly feel about Mary Ann."

"Yes, I know you didn't, but you've got to understand my vocabulary and grammar do not work well together at finding the right words. When they don't come together at a time like this, I can't express my true feelings. This is especially after my first relationship ended. You know Sue, that may be one of the reasons behind my failed relationship, not being able to express my own true feelings."

"Yes, you could be right. I find myself sometimes in the same situation of not knowing the right words to say, and when to say them, for they don't seem to come out all that easy anymore."

"Like right now there is so much I would love to say to you but knowing my best friend has already told you that she's in love with you as well. Oh, if only you knew how my heart hurts so deeply to take you into my arms and tell you how I truly feel. However, I can't, because I know that you have also told her how you feel. Who am I to stand in the way of my best friend being happy again?"

"Oh Sue, are you okay? You look like you're in another world?"

"Oh, I'm sorry, I was just thinking about a time not so long ago. Clay, do you remember when we first met here at this coffeeshop, and I was going through my divorce?"

"Yes, I do, so why do you ask?"

"No particular reason. I was only thinking back to when we first met, that's all."

"Yes, you're right, it was not that long ago that we met here in this coffee shop. Do you recall when the captain slapped you on your behind? "

"Yes Clay, I remember him doing that and I wanted to say something so bad but at the same time, I didn't want to lose my job here. It was the only income I had. You know that deadbeat ex-husband wasn't helping pay any of the bills."

" Sue, I'm sorry, I didn't mean to bring up harsh memories of the past."

"No, it wasn't you that brought up my ex-husband's past."

"Well, before I go, may I ask you one last question?"

"It depends on what kind of question you want to ask me."

"Wait, what do you think I'm about to ask you?" Clay chuckles.

"Clay, is it going to be a personal question or just a general question?"

"I guess you could say it's a personal question, does it really matter?"

"Well, no but being that it's you, I guess it's okay to go ahead with your question."

"Okay, here is my question. If you ever found yourself in the predicament of having two people telling you that they both have strong feelings for you, how would you handle the situation? Now you must remember that one of them gave you an ultimatum that didn't sit well with you. The other person told you they just wanted you to be happy no matter who you choose to be with."

"Hmm Clay, before I answer that let me ask you something. Could you live with a person who may make your life a living nightmare by giving you an ultimatum in every aspect of the relationship or would you rather be with someone who is willing to just see you be happy?"

"Sue, I should have known you would turn the tables on me."

"Well then, it's a no-brainer. I would choose the one who has my best interests at heart, and I'll leave it at that. You must make the choice, not me."

"Well, thank you for pointing that out. I should head over to Gloria's and get this over with. Sue, how much do I owe for four cups of coffee?"

"You don't owe anything for the coffee, it's on me."

"Are you sure?" Sue replied.

"Yes Clay, I'm sure. Now go and let Gloria down easily." On Sue's mind "and try not to break her heart as badly as you have mine."

"Well thank you Sue, that's very kind of you. I left you a tip on the table."

"Bye Clay!"

"Bye, I'll see you later. That is if Gloria doesn't kill me first."

Sue laughs and replies: "Oh Clay, I don't think Gloria is going to kill you… but who am I to say how a scorned woman might react to a man's rejection?"

Sue laughed. "Yes, Sue, that's what I'm afraid of. Just how will she respond to the letdown?"

"Well Clay, if we don't see you in a few days, we'll know where to send the police to look for you". Sue chuckles.

"Haha, very funny Sue, bye."

"Bye Clay and good luck letting Gloria down."

"Thanks, Sue, I'll see you later, I hope."

Sue then turned her attention to one of her co-workers.

"Hey Kim, you got a minute?"

"Sure Sue, what do you need?"

"I need you to take over for me. I got an errand to run."

"Sure, Sue I can, but for how long will you be gone?"

"It all depends on how long it's going to take me to get there and back. Now no more questions; I got to go!!"

"Well then be careful. Boy I tell you, I wonder about her sometimes."
Kim thought to herself.

"Hello, Sir, how was your meal?"

"Ma'am it was one of the best steaks and loaded potatoes I've had
in a long time! I'll be eating here more often for sure!"

"Thank you for the compliment. Your total is forty-five dollars
and eighty-two cents." "Wait ma'am that can't be right, I only
had ten oz. steak and loaded potato."

"Yes sir, I know but you must understand the price of things has
gone way up."

"Well ma'am, I guess I won't be eating here again if things are
that expensive."

"Well sir, I'm sorry you feel that way, but it's your prerogative to
choose where you eat."

Time to Face Gloria

As I make my way to Gloria's apartment door, I hear laughter coming from within her apartment. I knocked on the door and to my surprise there was a strange man who answered the door. I asked if this was Ms. Gloria's apartment, he replied "yes." I answered "well there for a second sir, I thought I was in the wrong apartment."

"Sir. Would you like to come in?"

As I step in the door, I pause thinking. I'm not sure if I should be doing this or not, but I'm needing to talk with Gloria.

"Sir, she's back in the bedroom getting dressed for our date tonight. We're going to see this new movie that she has been wanting to see."

"Oh, okay then will you tell her that I came by to see her?"

"Sure, I'll let her know, but first I need your name."

"Oh yes, just tell her that Clay came by, and who are you?"

"Oh, I'm sorry Clay, I'm Gloria's fiancé Paul."

I wonder if I understood him correctly when he said he was Gloria's fiancé.

"Clay, I just got back into town yesterday. I don't know if Gloria told you about me or not, but see I have this job that keeps me going three to four months at a time".

"No, I can't say she ever mentions your name Paul, but congratulations, you're one lucky man to have Gloria!"

"Thanks Clay, I've been waiting long enough for her to accept my proposal. Now Clay may I ask why you're needing to talk with Gloria?"

"Paul, it's nothing of great importance. It can wait another day."

"Clay, if you are needing to speak with her it needs to be tonight, because tomorrow morning we'll be flying back to Australia to plan our June wedding."

"That's great Paul, there's no need for you to say anything to her about me stopping by then."

"Why is that Clay? Is there something I need to know?"

"Oh no Paul there's nothing at all."

I'm thinking I need to end this conversation now before Gloria walks in and sees us talking.

"Paul it was nice to have met you, and good luck to you both at your wedding; now I must be going, are I'll be late for my dinner date with Mary Ann."

"Well Clay it was nice meeting you as well, goodbye". I realize just how awkward that was as I leave the apartment complex. She had never told me about being engaged to a man as big as Paul. I would say he stands about 6" foot and a half and is built like a muscular bodybuilder.

I'm hoping he doesn't say anything to her about me stopping by or even asking her how she knows me. Because if he ever finds out, I feel he may just come looking for me, and that would not be good for him or me. I'm just glad I didn't take her up on her offer down at the beach Monday night.

I can now tell Mary Ann that everything went smoothly tonight. As I make my way to Mary Ann for dinner, there appears this voice asking Clay "are you sure that's what you're going to tell her?"

"Wait, now we're not going to play this game again."

"Who said anything about me not being truthful?"

"Clay did you not just say everything went smoothly at Gloria's, as I recall you didn't even speak with her?"

"Hmm, yeah, you got me there. What else can I say?"

"Well Clay, my advice is you first tell her that you met Gloria's fiancé and go from there". "Hmm, I guess that will work. Wait, I got a better idea."

"What idea would that be?"

"What if I just keep my mouth shut and don't say anything about me going over to Gloria's?"

"Now Clay!! You know that's not going to work. Mary Ann will ask you all kinds of questions."

"I have a question for you. Will you stop annoying me: for this situation will work itself out in due time?"

"Well excuse me! Clay, I was only trying to help; but if that's the way you feel then okay goodbye!!!"

"Goodbye"

Now on to Mary Ann's.

Dinner with Mary Ann

As I make my way up to the front door of Mary Ann's house, I smell the mixed aroma of turnip greens, fried chicken and cornbread coming from her kitchen. Now there is also a hint of what could be peach cobbler. I'm thinking back to what Mr. John said earlier and that's what Mrs. Mary is cooking for dinner tonight. I'm starting to wonder just whose house I'm at now understand today has been a long one for me. I'm just going to knock on the door and see who answers.

"Knock, knock". I wait and wait some more as I look at my watch. I'm thinking maybe I should try Mrs. Mary's knocking technique. Just as I go to knock, the door opens and there before me stands a beautiful, shaped silhouette of a woman wearing nothing but this midnight blue sleeping shirt. "Well Clay, are you going to just stand there gazing or are you coming in?"

"Oh, I'm sorry, yes thank you, and then the door closed behind me. "Clay, I was beginning to wonder if you had forgotten about our dinner plans tonight. I hope you like what I've fixed for tonight."

"Oh, I'm sure I will be Mary Ann."

"Please come on into the kitchen, I've got everything sitting on the table awaiting". "Wow, Mary Ann, I wasn't expecting a candlelight dinner with red cabernet sauvignon. May I ask where you found it?"

"I ordered it straight from one of the vineyards over in southern France."

"That must have cost you a fortune."

"No, not really Clay. I have this friend who's from there that I went to college with."

"Oh, I see. Please tell me more about your friend."

"Well, she and I had made plans to open our own mental health practice together after college."

"Now I'm starting to understand why you said what you did at the beach, but I thought..."

"Wait Clay let me finish. There is more to the story than just that part."

"Oh, I'm sorry please continue."

"Well one day after our first class or was it during our second class that she got this phone call saying one of her brothers had become ill; and she was needed back home right away."

"Did she ever say what was wrong with him?"

"She may have, but I've forgotten, for that all took place during our senior year."

"Don't you both stay in touch?"

"Yes, but not like we once did. Not long after her beloved brother had passed away, she called me saying that she was going to stay and help her family run their vineyard business. Now that I think about it, it has been a very long time since we have spoken to one another. I need to see if I can find her phone number and give her a call."

"Yes, you need to do it for old time sakes and speaking of time, I need to head on back to Mr. Johns before it gets later."

"Wait Clay, you haven't told me how your talk went with Gloria this afternoon. Now you did go to her place and tell her about us, right?"

"Yes Mary Ann, I did, but I didn't get to speak with her, because her fiancé answered the door."

"Did I understand you to say her fiancé?"

"Yes, you did, and his name is Paul. You should have seen him. I'm telling you, he stands six feet and a half, and is built like a bodybuilder. Now as he's telling me this, I'm thinking to myself it would be in my best interest not to say anything about Gloria's ultimatum and just forget about talking to her. Now why are you laughing?"

"I would love to have been there to see the look on your face when he told you that he was her fiancé."

"Well, it was a shocking event for me that's for sure; I didn't know what to say next to him."

"Clay, Sue and I could have told you a thing or two about her, but we felt you needed to find out about her for yourself."

"Well, Mary Ann, to be honest I'm feeling a little confused as to why you both didn't say anything to me about her."

"Clay, let me try to explain the situation in a way which you will understand."

"Okay I'm listening."

"Clay from my and Sue's viewpoint as women, we feel it's not our place to destroy another woman's character; although there are some women out there who will just out of pure anger."

"Mary Ann, you've made this a very special night for me. It's one I won't forget anytime soon."

"How is that Clay?"

"Mary Ann, you've once again shown me a side of yourself that I've never seen before in a woman. For you're most definitely unlike any other woman I've ever met before."

"Clay, I can assure you, you haven't seen me yet. There's a lot more to come."

"Oh, will you look at the time? I need to be going."

"Who's to say that you got to be going, I'm not?"

Hmm, decisions, decisions; I'm thinking do I go, or do I stay to see what's to come, for which will it be? Then all at once I hear a soft voice saying remember the Lord's prayer.

"Mary Ann, where is your Bible?"

"Clay it's in my bedroom on the nightstand where I keep it. Why would you like me to get it?"

"Yes, please do. I need to find out a few things.

"Okay I'll go get it, if you don't mind fixing us a cup of coffee and meeting me back in the living room."

"Sure, I can handle that; what would you like in your coffee?"

"Clay, you know how I like my coffee?"

"All right, then I'll drink my coffee black."

"Now, what are you looking for in the Bible?"

"Mary Ann to be completely honest with you from the time you opened your door, I've felt tempted by your illustrious beauty, and I became even more so seeing your eyes sparkling by the flicking candle light. Your beauty has once again taken me over unto a place that I'm not sure I'm ready for yet again."

"Clay, your words are very sweet, thank you. Now can you tell me what you're looking for?"

"Okay, I've found it. Here you can read the Lord's prayer starting with verse 9". (K.J.V.) Matthew Chapter 6, verses 9-through-13. Read as follows. "After this manner therefore pray ye: Our Father which art in heaven, Hallowed be thy name. Thy kingdom comes. Thy will be done on earth, as it is in heaven. Give us this day our daily bread. And forgive us for our debts, as we forgive our debtors. And lead us not into temptation but deliver us from evil: For thine is the kingdom, power, and glory, forever. Amen".)

"Now Mary Ann in my present situation which I've found myself in tonight: I'm putting more emphasis on verse 13 for what it says, "And lead us not into temptation but deliver us from evil."

"Clay, are you saying I'm evil in some way?"

"No way Mary Ann, I'm not saying that at all. What I am saying is that the lust that comes with temptation is so evil."

"Clay, are you always tempted by my beauty?"

"Mary Ann, you had to ask me that question. Let me turn to what Paul has to say in Romans Chapter 7 reading verses 15 through 20 for they read as forwards. (I don't understand what I'm doing. For what I will do, I do not practice; but what I hear, that I do. If then, I do what I will not do, I agree with the law that it is good.

But now, it is no longer I who do it, but sin that dwells in me. For I know that in me (that is, in my flesh) nothing good dwells; for to will is present in me, but how to perform what is good I do not find. For the good that I will do, I do not do; but the evil that I will not do, I practice. Now if I do what I will not do, it is no longer I who does it, but sin that dwells in me)."

"Now Mary Ann, does that help to answer your question?"

"Yes, Clay does it in a way, but I'm not sure I'm understanding this in the way you do."

Oh boy! How do I explain this in a way that she will understand?

"Mary Ann, I'm not a biblical philosopher, but I'm going to say in my way of thinking what Paul is saying is that the things we should not do, we sometimes find ourselves doing, and the good things we should be doing, we sometimes find ourselves not doing as we should. Now does that make any sense to you at all?"

"Yes Clay, I think I understand it more now that you put it in your own words. But I don't feel you've answered my question fully."

Let me think this over before I answer her in a different way and hope that she'll understand.

"Mary Ann, being a man who has strong affections and needs for a woman, I'll tell you that I'll always be tempted by your beauty. However, that doesn't mean I need to fall into bed with you."

"Now Clay, why didn't you just come out and say that in the first place?"

Hmm, I'm thinking to myself that if she doesn't know why, I'm not going to explain it again. I'll say goodnight.

"Clay, would you like another cup of coffee?"

"No ma'am, I must say goodnight now you're okay with me coming by tomorrow morning. I'll have a cup with you then."

"Clay, you know you're always welcome here."

Thank you, and I'll walk with you to the coffee shop in the morning before I go to the cemetery."

"Clay before you go, may I get at least one goodnight kiss?"

I'm thinking "hmm" I don't know if I can handle one kiss with the way you're looking standing there in that midnight blue sleeping shirt halfway up your thighs. However, I guess it will be okay this time.

"Yes, you may."

"Goodnight Clay sweet dreams my love". Sweet dreams for you too, my lovely lady. I'll see you in the early hours of the morning.

Back to Mr. John's

As I walk back to Mr. John's. I start to wonder what is going to happen if they sell the motorcycle shop and start their traveling around the world, just where would that leave me? Where am I going to stay and what will I do for a living? For there are many unknown questions, I don't know the answer. Maybe Mrs. Mary will come up with something tomorrow that will help me solve these questions, she has before. But knowing her like I do, she might suggest moving in with her daughter Lana. I think that idea wouldn't sit well with me or Lana.

Here's an idea that might work. What if his sons take the remaining inventory of the shop; then I could buy it for myself? Oh wait, there's that annoying voice again.

"Now Clay, what are you going to do with the shop and how do you think you can get the money to buy it, if he decides to sell it to you?"

"Hmm," more questions to answer. First thing first, we need to wait and see if they're still considering selling the shop.

"Oh, they're going to sell it all right, John has decided about that."

"How can you know that for certain? For you don't even know what will happen with the two investigators when they show up Monday morning."

"Oh, right I'd forgotten about them two coming back."

"Now I see you don't know everything like you think you do. Now you can see your way out. "

I got some serious thinking to do. As I walk through the front door, I see Mrs. Mary reading her Bible.

"Well hello Mrs. Mary, I wasn't expecting you to still be up."

"Hi, Clay, I wasn't sleepy yet, so I decided to catch up on my reading of First Corinthians in Chapter seven. Now come over here and tell me how your meeting with Gloria went?

I thought it funny that she had asked about Gloria and not Mary Ann.

"Well to be honest my meeting with Gloria didn't happen, nor will it happen in the future."

"Why what happened?"

"Mrs. Mary, all I can say is that I learned a lot more about her today. When I knocked on her apartment door her fiancé answered."

"Do what?Wait a minute, did I understand you to say fiancé?"

"Yes ma'am, can we change the subject please?"

"Sure, what would you like to talk about?"

"Mrs. Mary, you said you were reading First Corinthians, Chapter Seven in the K.J.V., just how does it start off?"

"Here Clay, you can read it for yourself, if you can read."

"Oh, aren't you funny tonight?"

"Well yes, I am, Clay, but on a more serious note, I've been wanting to ask you something for some time now."

"Mrs. Mary, what would that be?"

"Clay, why don't you carry the Bible to church with you?"

"Wow, I didn't see that question coming, but it's a good question just the same. Mrs. Mary, as you well know, our preacher preaches from the N.I.V., for it doesn't read just like the K.J.V. that I'm used to hearing preachers preach from so now you know."

"Okay that makes sense, I guess."

"Okay thank you, now here's what it says in the KJV".

"First Corinthians, Chapter Seven "Now concerning the things ye wrote unto me: It is good for a man not to touch a woman. Nevertheless, to avoid fornication, let every man have his own wife, and let every woman have her own husband."

"Mrs. Mary, I really needed to read this tonight, thank you."

"You're welcome, Clay. Now I'm off to say goodnight. We'll talk more in the morning, or one more thing before I go: you are coming over to Lana's for lunch tomorrow right?"

"Yes ma'am, that's my plan, *if I don't forget my way there*" Goodnight!"

A Saturday Night Dream

As I lay here in bed trying to fall asleep. I begin to toss and turn because I can't stop thinking about how beautiful Mary Ann looked sitting there in the candlelight as we ate dinner. As my eyes close into deep sleep, I envision what may have happened had I stayed the night.

"Mary Ann, are you sure you are okay with me spending the night here on the couch for the night?"

"Yes, Clay, I'm sure it will be alright for tonight; but don't you think you would be more comfortable sleeping on the bed in the guest room rather than lying on the couch? "

"Yes, I believe I would, but I must warn you; I've been told I snore. "

"Oh, if your snoring gets too loud, I have some earplugs to sleep with."

"Okay Mary Ann, it's your call.

"Clay, believe me everything is going to be fine, now don't worry it's only one night."

I'm thinking my snoring is not what I'm mostly worried about here, it's more about us ending up in the same bed together. All at once I felt something rubbing against my legs. I opened my eyes to see what it could be; it was only Mrs. Mary, who had come back into the living room.

"Sorry Clay, I didn't mean to wake you. I saw that you had fallen asleep here on the couch; I thought I would put this blanket over you."

"Oh, it's okay Mrs. Mary, I was dreaming."

"May I ask what you were dreaming about?"

"I was telling Mary Ann about the time Mr. John banged on the bedroom door screaming wake-up in there you're snoring is keeping us awake, that's when I felt you putting the blanket over me. "

"Well, I am sorry to have woken you up from your dream. "

"No ma'am it's all good; I'll just fall asleep in my bed. This old couch has gotten very uncomfortable to sleep on."

As I make my way to my bedroom, I'm thinking now if that doesn't sound just like the way my life story has unfolded over the past seven years, I don't know what does. No sooner than my head hit the pillar, the lights went out.

"Sunday Morning"

I woke up around four-thirty this morning to go to the bathroom. On my way there I heard Mr. John and Mrs. Mary in the kitchen talking. I can't make out what they're saying. However, it sounds like they're discussing how they'll tell their family today that they're planning to sell the shop and home to travel.

Once I'm done with my shower, I get dressed and walk into the kitchen and say good morning to them both. Mrs. Mary answered, "Good morning, Clay. You're up early."

"Yes, ma'am I'm at that. I have a lot to get done if I'm hoping to make it to Lana's today for lunch."

"Clay, would you like me to fix you something to eat before you get your day started?"

"No thanks Mrs. Mary, I've told Mary Ann that I'd stop by the coffee shop for breakfast. I'll see you both later."

"Okay Clay see you later."

"John, I can help but wonder sometimes what's going on within that mind."

"Mary, I've told you more than once that he doesn't have a brain to think with; I believe when God says here's a brain for you, Clay thought He said rain and ran for shelter."

"Well then John, I'm guessing you must have gotten a double portion, because what you've just said does not make sense. Would you like another biscuit to enjoy with your eggs and rice?

"Yes, ma'am and may I also have another glass of milk please?

"John, you know the more I think about us selling out and traveling around the world the more excited I become about it."

"Yes, Mary, I am looking forward to it, but I don't know how the family will react to us telling them."

"John, I've just thought about this. Where is Clay going to stay once we sell everything?" "Mary, he is a grown man. I'm sure he can find a place to live and work; for he's not our problem to worry about."

"John, that's no way to think about someone who has become like family."

"Mary, I'm sorry but that's the way I feel. We have our own family to consider here."

"John, I'm sorry you feel that way. I'll figure out some way to help him before the end of the day."

"Well, Mary, don't expect me to help you."

"Oh, you hard-headed old goat, I won't even think of asking you for help; I can handle this on my own: now are you going to help me clean the kitchen before we go?"

"That my love, I don't mind helping you with. Where would you like me to start?"

Sunday walk to Mary Anna's

As I was walking to Mary Ann's this morning, I began to reflect on what was running through my mind last night as I walked back to Mr. John's. Now if they sold their home and let me rent the shop, I could open a western wear store of my own. I finally make it to Mary Ann's front porch; and as I start up the steps one gives away causing my left ankle to twist, which prompts me to yell, which causes Mary Ann to come to the door.

" Good morning Mary Ann, you look lovely this morning."

"Good morning, Clay. Are you okay? I heard you yell."

"Yes, I think so. One of the steps just broke causing my ankle to twist really badly, but I don't think it's broken."

"Clay, let me help you in, and I'll take a look at it. Now sit here and take off your left boot."

"Mary Ann, I'm sorry but you're going to have to take it off for me. It's hurting pretty badly."

"Okay Clay, can you pick up your leg for me?"

"I'll try, but man this is not the way I wanted my day to start out."

"Clay, can you wiggle your ankle for me?"

"No, it hurts too bad to move it."

"Is it impossible for you to move it even a bit?"

"No, I can't. Can you not see how badly it has swollen in just this short period of time?"

"I'm not a nurse or doctor, so I'm going to take you to the hospital to look at."

"Yes, ma'am I agree with you; but before we leave may I use your phone to contact Mrs. Mary to let her know what has happened?"

"Yes, you may."

"Hello Mr. John, it's Clay."

"Yes, I know who you are. Now why are you calling?"

"Well!! Mr. John, I'm calling to let you and Mrs. Mary know I've twisted my ankle, and it looks like I may have broken it. Mary Ann is bringing me to the hospital to have a doctor check it."

"Okay we'll be at Lana's, so let us know what the doctor says, bye."

"John, what is wrong with Clay? Why is he taken to the hospital?"

"He just twisted his ankle, and Mary Ann thinks it's broken; (I wonder if he didn't break his neck instead.)"

"Did John say how it happened?"

"No, he didn't, Mary, not that it matters to me."

"I'm hoping he's okay and still able to see Lana."

"I have everything loaded in the car Mary, if you're ready let's go."

"Yes, John, I'm ready."

Visit to the E. R.

"Mary Ann, did I tell you that Mr. and Mrs. John have decided to sell their home and shop?"

"No, Clay, you haven't. When did they decide on that?"

"I guess maybe a week or so ago."

"Wait, Clay, are you sure of this?"

"Yes, I overheard Mr. John telling Mrs. Mary that he's fallen three months behind on his monthly payments for the shop's parts. The only thing he knows how to do is sell out. Now if they do this I'm not sure where or what I'll do."

"Well, Clay, we can talk about this later, okay, let's get you in here and let the doctor look at your ankle. Now you stay put, and I'll get a wheelchair".

I'm thinking, "Yeah, it doesn't look like I'll be going anywhere on this ankle".

"Excuse me nurse, may I use this wheelchair? I've got a friend outside who hurt his left ankle."

"Yes, ma'am, but I must tell you up-front that once you bring him through those doors, there's some paperwork he will need to figure out before the doctor can check his ankle."

"Yes ma'am, I'll let him know that."

"Well, Mary Ann, you sure took your sweet time getting back in the chair. I could've crawled in there faster."

"Clay stop complaining and just get in the chair because the nurse said that you will need to figure out these papers before you can see the doctor."

"Yes ma'am; now Mary Ann do you have homeowners' property insurance?"

"Yes, why do you ask that?"

"Here it's asking, did this accident occur on someone's property other than your own, if so, does the owner of the property have insurance?"

"Clay, I don't have that information with me, so say no."

"If I answer no, I am sure they will ask how I will pay for this visit."

"Clay, just tell them to bill you. I need to call Sue to let her know I'm going to be late to work."

"Okay, I'll tell them to send you the bill."

Uh-oh, I guess it looks like today is not going to be one of my best days at all. There's Mrs. Mary's daughter Lana. I wonder why she's here this morning.

"Hello Lana, why are you here this morning?"

"Clay, I was about to ask you that very same question, but since you asked first, I've worked the night shift this week. Now what are you doing here?"

"Lana, I've twisted my ankle, and Mary Ann thought I needed to have it looked at by a doctor."

"Well, let me see, oh that does look bad; the doctor will be in shortly to look at it: now in the meantime can I get you anything?"

"No ma'am, but before you go, what time are you getting off?"

"I got another half hour; why do you ask?"

"Well, Mary Ann has to get to work, so I was thinking since you're here maybe I could get a ride with you". "Oh, sure Clay; I'd be more than happy to give you a ride home."

"Thank you, I'll let Mary Ann know, so she doesn't have to wait."

"Okay."

"Good morning Mr. Clay, I'm Dr. Frank. Could you please tell me what you've done to your left ankle?" "Doctor, I twisted it climbing up the steps."

"I don't believe it's broken, so I'll say it's just a sprain."

"Doctor, aren't you planning to do an X-ray to be sure?"

"I see no need for it while it's swollen, so I recommend soaking it in hot water and Epsom salt three times a day. I also recommend you wrap it up with an ace bandage and use these crutches and wear these boots when you are not using them. Now you need to do this for a week, and if it's not any better at the end of the week you come back to see me, and I'll do an X-ray".

"I sure will, Doctor."

As I make my way back to the waiting room to find Mary Ann, I'm thinking to myself, thanks for nothing Dr. Frankenstein, I could've made that diagnosis on my own.

"Lana, have you seen Mary Ann?"

"Yes Clay, and I told her you were riding home with me, so she left about twenty minutes ago."

I'm ready if you are". "Okay I'll bring the car around to the E.R. doors, so you don't have to walk that far."

"Thanks Lana."

Lana's Home

Lana, I can't thank you enough for letting me ride back home with you."

"Oh, Clay, it's alright. I'm glad I was still at work when you came into the emergency room. Did mom tell you what we're having for lunch today?"

"No, I cannot say she did."

"Well for dessert we will have banana pudding, and I'm thinking Lawrence said his wife was fixing a red velvet cake."

"Wait, who is Lawrence again?"

"Clay, have you forgotten who Lawrence is? He's my baby brother."

"Oh, that's right, I met him last year at your mother's birthday party."

"They're here, we've been waiting for you to arrive. Clay, what did the doctor say about your ankle?"

"Mrs. Mary, he said it's only a bad sprain, I need to soak it in hot water and Epsom salt three times a day for a week."

"Lana,   do   you   have   any   Epsom   salt?"
"Yes, ma'am it's in the bathroom along with the bath-pan."

"Clay, you can take a seat on the couch while I get this fixed for you."

"Thank you, Mrs. Mary, for doing this for me."

"Clay, it's my pleasure to help you. Now sit back and get comfortable. I'll be back shortly."

"Mr. John, now that the women aren't in the room, there's something I'd like to ask you." "Clay, what's your question?"

"Mr. John, I've been thinking if you and Mrs. Mary sell your motorcycle shop and home; would you let me buy just the shop?"

"Now Clay, if we sold you the shop, what would you do with it?"

"Mr. John, I would turn into a western wear store, with a Danish pastry and coffee shop on the other end."

"Clay, where're you going to get that kind of money to do that?"

"Mr. John, don't you worry about that, for I have a way of getting the money. Now will you let me buy the shop?"

"Well, I'll talk it over with Mary and my two sons and let you know. Now I'm going to see if Mary and Lana need help in the kitchen."

"Before you go, would you hand me my notebook and pen, please sir?"

"Sure Mr. Clay; now will there be anything else you'll be needing?"

"No, sir but thanks for asking."

Oh, my Lord, I don't understand why Mr. John has been so rude to me here lately; have I done something wrong to him that I don't know about? I guess the only way I'll find out is to come right out and ask him.

"Clay, would you like me to fix you a plate or do you want to come in here and dine with us?"

"Lana, if you don't mind, I'll eat here; start soaking my foot in this hot water."

"Okay, I'll bring our plates in here, so you don't have to eat alone.

"That would be very kind of you Lana, thank you. Lana, once we're done eating would you like to take a walk with me down by the ocean?"

"Clay, you're on crutches and want to walk down to the ocean; have you lost your mind?"

"Lana, I can answer that for you. He never had a mind to lose."

"Now Mr. John, I don't know what I've done to you, for you to say things like that. However, I'm getting sick and tired of hearing those kinds of remarks coming from you."

"Yes, John, so am I. Now either you tell him what he has done, or you stop saying things like that about him."

"Okay, Mary, you're right; Clay, I'm sorry for talking down about you; you might have a brain after all, and no you haven't done anything wrong, for I've only been joking around."

"Thank you, Mr. John. Those words mean a lot, but I don't feel your apology is sincere."

"Well, Clay, I'm not going to get down on my knees and say I'm sorry if that's what you're thinking."

"No, Mr. John, that's not at all what I'm thinking, for I wouldn't ask any person to do that". "Good because I'm not."

"You know Mr. John, there's one way you can show me that you're sincere."

"Oh, yeah how's that Clay?"

"Rent me the motorcycle shop for two years and after those two years are up and if I've made a substantial profit, you can sell it to me."

"John, why are you scratching your head?"

"Well, Mary, I think he may solve both of our problems."

"How is that?"

"Mary, you told me on the way here that he would need a place to live."

"Well, Mr. John, does that mean you'll do it?"

"Yes Clay, I'll be willing to rent you the shop, only if my sons are okay with it, but it can only be for one year not two."

"Thank you, Mr. John, you as well Mrs. Mary. I'll try my best not to disappoint either of you."

"Clay, I've got one question for you. Are you going to keep selling motorcycles?"

'No, Mrs. Mary, I'm not. I'm going to open a western shop and call it Clay's Western Wear."

"Hmm, Clay's western wear sounds very nice doesn't it, Lana?"

Well, I guess it does, mom if you're into that kind of stuff, which you know I'm not."

"Oh, well then, Clay, would you like a bowl of my homemade banana pudding?"

"Yes Mrs. Mary, that would be nice thank you."

"Lana, would you mind reading this and telling me if you think it's any good or not?"

"Sure Clay, I'll be glad to read it."

"A Dark Road"

As I once again find myself going down this dark road in life looking for peace that I can't find in this evil world, I begin to pray oh my Lord where can I find this peace that I'm looking for? As I continue to walk all alone in the darkness of my sin searching for peace, I see in the far distance what appears to be a small dim light; for the light reminds me of the darkness of my sinful life. I find myself standing before this altar with my eyes closed. I kneel for my heart's eyes begging to open for the first time. I see the image of Jesus' face appear before me as He hung up on that old wooden cross meant for a sinner like me, seeing His blood as it ran down His face; I'm reminded of these words He spoke that day as He hung on that cross. He cried out saying.

("Father, forgive them; for they do not know what they're doing"). (K.J.V. - Luke 23:34).

"Wow, Clay, I must say that's very impressive.

"Thank you, Lana. Now read this one and tell me what you think about it."

"Wait, don't tell me, you have written another one. When do you find time to write?"

"Now Mr. John, don't you say anything?"

"Clay, I wasn't going to."

"Yeah, right. I bet you weren't a hard-headed old goat."

"Lana, I mostly do all my writing at night, because it is more peaceful."

"Well okay Clay let me see what you've written."

Jesus walk the Line

Jesus walked that straight and narrow path, that no one could ever walk on the day He was crucified. For He took up that old heavy cross meant for you and me that day. Jesus knew we couldn't carry the weight of our sins on our own. He therefore walked the straight line in our place taking the sins of this evil world upon His bloody back. Oh my, Lord, my savior, where do I begin to thank You for our salvation, which You gave so freely unto us all through Your blood which You shed on that day in which You were crucified in our place?

"Now Clay, I don't mean to say it the wrong way, but this one does not appeal to me as much as the first one did."

"Why is that Lana?"

"Clay, I really don't know how to explain it. It just sounds all wrong and missing something, but I don't know what that something is; maybe it's all in the way you got it worded."

"Well thank you for taking a look at it and giving me your honest opinion. I'll take it back and rewrite it then your mother can read over it once I'm done."

"Well Clay, are you going to let me read it? Maybe I can tell you what's wrong with it?"

"Mr. John, you've never liked anything I've written."

"Clay, you know that's not true, don't you recall that time you wrote that screenplay? Didn't I tell you, I like it."

"Well, that's the only time you even said you liked anything I've written. Now that I think back, it seems that I recall hearing you tell Mrs. Mary that you believe she wrote that, now did you not?"

"Yes, I did say that Clay, but she said she didn't, so I believe her. Now you got anything else to say?"

"No, Sir, but there is something that I would like to ask you all before we go."

"Okay Clay, what's on your mind that can't wait until tomorrow?"

"Mr. John, I feel you all understand the Bible better than I do; so, my question is this: what does it mean by not relying on your own understanding?"

"Hmm, that's a great question. Lana, would you like to give us your answer first?"

"Gee thanks Mr. John, I don't mind if I do. Now, this is my interpretation of what it means. Now before I ever got saved, I didn't understand God's words, even though Dad and Mom took us to church every Sunday. It wasn't until I accepted Jesus as my savior and started studying His words that things become clearer for me. I said that to say this Clay, once you accept Jesus, you must let Him become your guide and rely on His wisdom and not your own."

"Lana, I understand somewhat where you are coming from, but I also feel there's more to it, now Mr. John it's your turn."

"Well, Clay after hearing what Lana had to say I don't know what else I could add other than this, once you've accepted our Lord as your savior, He gives to you His Holy Spirit which abides within you as He does all who have accepted His forgiveness and from

His Holy Spirit comes to understand. If you'd like, I'll show you here in my Bible K.J.V. where He's talking about this very subject."

"Oh, yes please do Mr. John. That would be a great ending for the chapter of this book."

"Wait did you say you're going to end this book with me reading from my Bible?"

"Yes Mr. John, I did."

"K.J.V. Proverbs.

Chapter 3 verse 3 through 7 reads as follows.

Let not mercy and truth forsake thee: bind them about thy neck; write them upon the table of thine heart: So shalt thou find favor and good understanding in the sight of God and man. Trust in the Lord with all thine heart; and lean not unto thine own understanding. In all thy ways acknowledge him, and he shall direct thy paths. Be not wise in thine own eyes: fear the Lord and depart from evil."

"Now Clay, do you have a better understanding of what it means not to rely on your own understanding of what the scripture teaches?"

"Mr. John, after hearing what you both had to say about your understanding of the scriptures, I'll say that I understand in a way. However, there's still something missing. Mr. Lawrence, would you like to share your thoughts?

"For my opinion doesn't matter. But I will share with you this out of the E.S.V book of Philippians 2:12-13 it reads ("Therefore, my beloved, as you have always obeyed, so now, not only in my presence but much more in my absence, work out your own salvation with fear and trembling, for it is God who works in you, both to will and to work for his good pleasure".)

"Now do you understand what these scriptures are saying?"

"Yes, I do believe so. Now Mrs. Mary, would you mind sharing your thoughts?"

"Yes, I would, Clay. I agree with Lawrence, and here's why. These are my own thoughts on this subject matter. I believe that before we were ever formed in the womb of our mother, God knew we would need a comforter in our daily walk. He therefore sent Jesus to be our guide. Does that make any sense to you?"

"I'll say this: you all gave some great answers. Now here's my take on your answers. Keep in mind this is my own opinion as well. I believe once someone has fullhearted accepted Jesus as their savior they become a born-again person, being filled with a moral understanding concerning knowing right from wrong. This knowledge can only come from obeying God. I feel the only way this will come about is by taking time to study His words and praying. For you must be sincere in asking for that understanding. For He knows if you're sincere or not."

The End

"Well, my friend, you've once again reached the end of another one of Clay's great adventures. I hope you have enjoyed these short stories as much as I have enjoyed sharing them with you. I'm signing out now. May God's blessing be with you, until we meet again.